Pretty Mouth

WRITTEN BY
BONES MCKAY

ILLUSTRATED BY
URSULA GRAY

www.PrettyMouthComic.com

ISBN: 978-1-9994044-4-4

FOR OUR READERS,
THANK YOU FOR ALL
OF YOUR SUPPORT.

I HAD STEAK... SO I'M PRETTY FULL.

GLANCE

YOU'RE FINE.

KISSU

NO, DON'T.

AW, EVAN, LET ME GET SOME *SUGAR.* HE'S A MONSTER, IT'S JUST FINE.

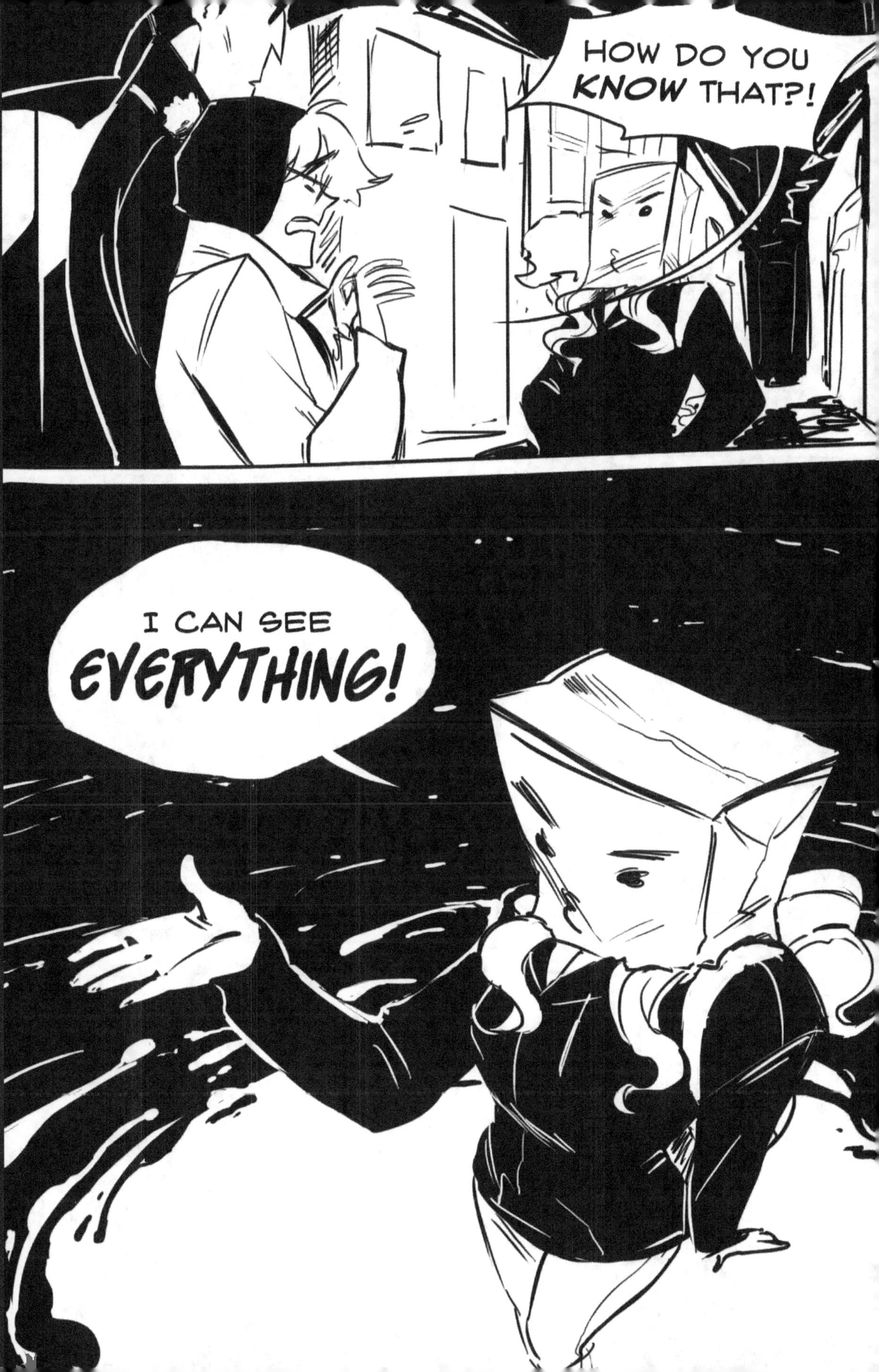
HOW DO YOU KNOW THAT?!
I CAN SEE EVERYTHING!

AND THIS GIRL.
THEY'RE BOTH CURSED I THINK...
AND I WAS WONDERING...
YOU WANT ME TO HELP THEM.
IF IT'S NOT TOO MUCH TROUBLE.
ARE THEY YOUR FRIENDS?

WELL, WHAT DO YOU WANT FROM ME?
I-I- DON'T HURT ME!
YOU'RE CURSED, CORRECT.

WHAT DO I DO?
THERE IS A BANISHED WITCH STEPPING OUTSIDE HER LINES. IF YOU SEND HER AWAY, I WILL HELP ALL THAT I CAN.

RING
RNG

I'M NOT
SEEING RIZO.

UH...
HI MOM...

IT'S STILL NOT
A GOOD TIME.

KNOCK
KNOCK

WAIT.
I'M RAMONA.
THANKS FOR TRYING TO HELP US OUT, RISOTTO.
OH.. I JUST LIKE TO HELP.
THAT'S MORE SWEET, SUGAR. YOU BE SAFE NOW, BIG GUY.
BYE RAMONA.

I KNOW EVERYTHING,

SAY IT.

WHAT?

JUST SAY IT, AND *I'LL CHANGE YOUR WORLD.*

NO, WHAT IS THAT?

SAY IT.

IS YOUR HAND OKAY?

YEAH IT'S FINE.

DID YOU FIND IRA?

I THINK SO. BUT WE'LL NEED DAD'S HELP.

RIGHT.

YOU HUNGRY?

YEAH.

I MEAN, I KNOW IT'LL HURT, I KNOW EVERYTHING.... BUT...
MAYBE MAKE IT QUICK. LIKE A BANDAID.
THOSE YOUR EYES?
LIKE A BANDAID.

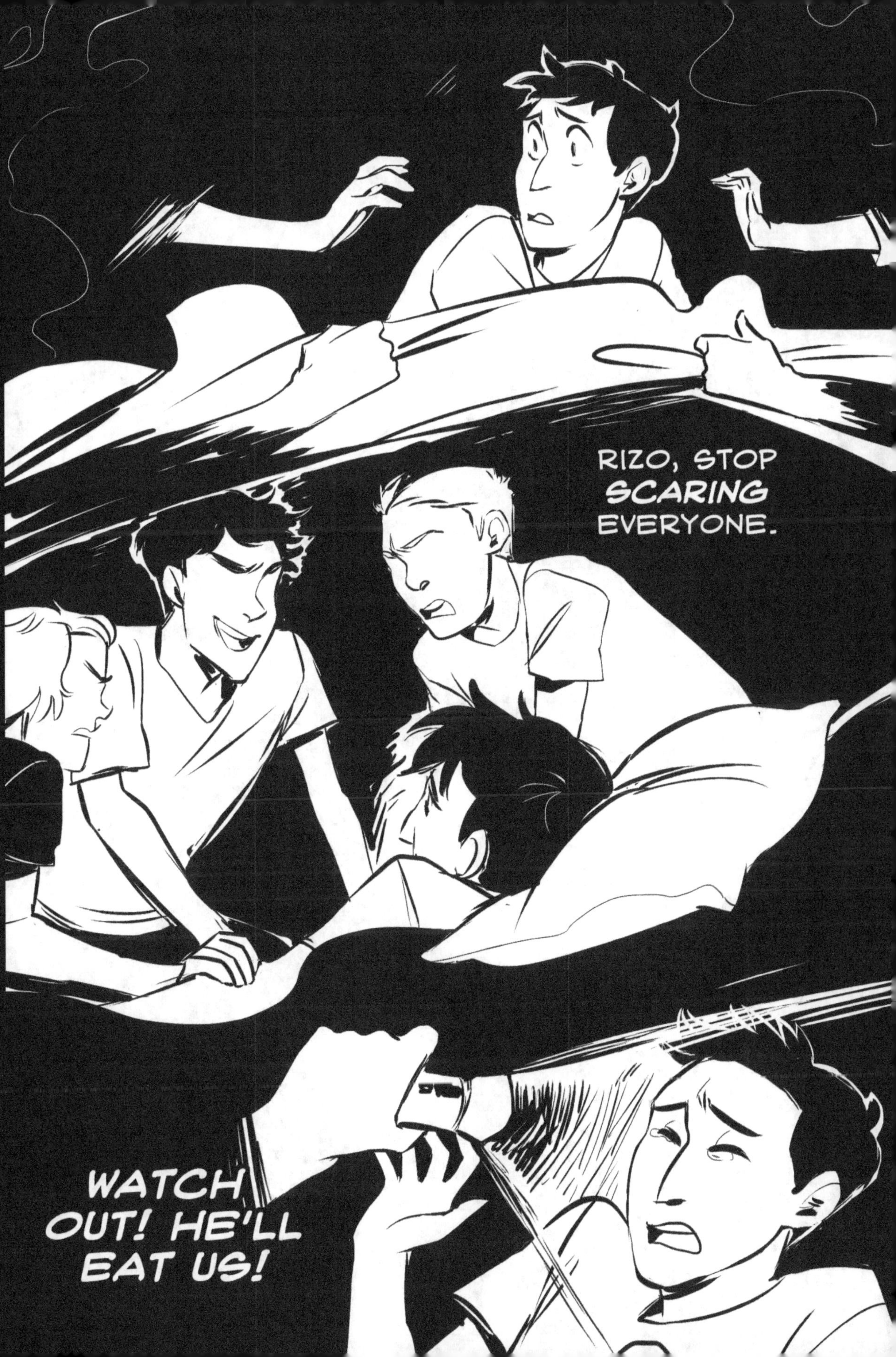
RIZO, STOP SCARING EVERYONE.
WATCH OUT! HE'LL EAT US!

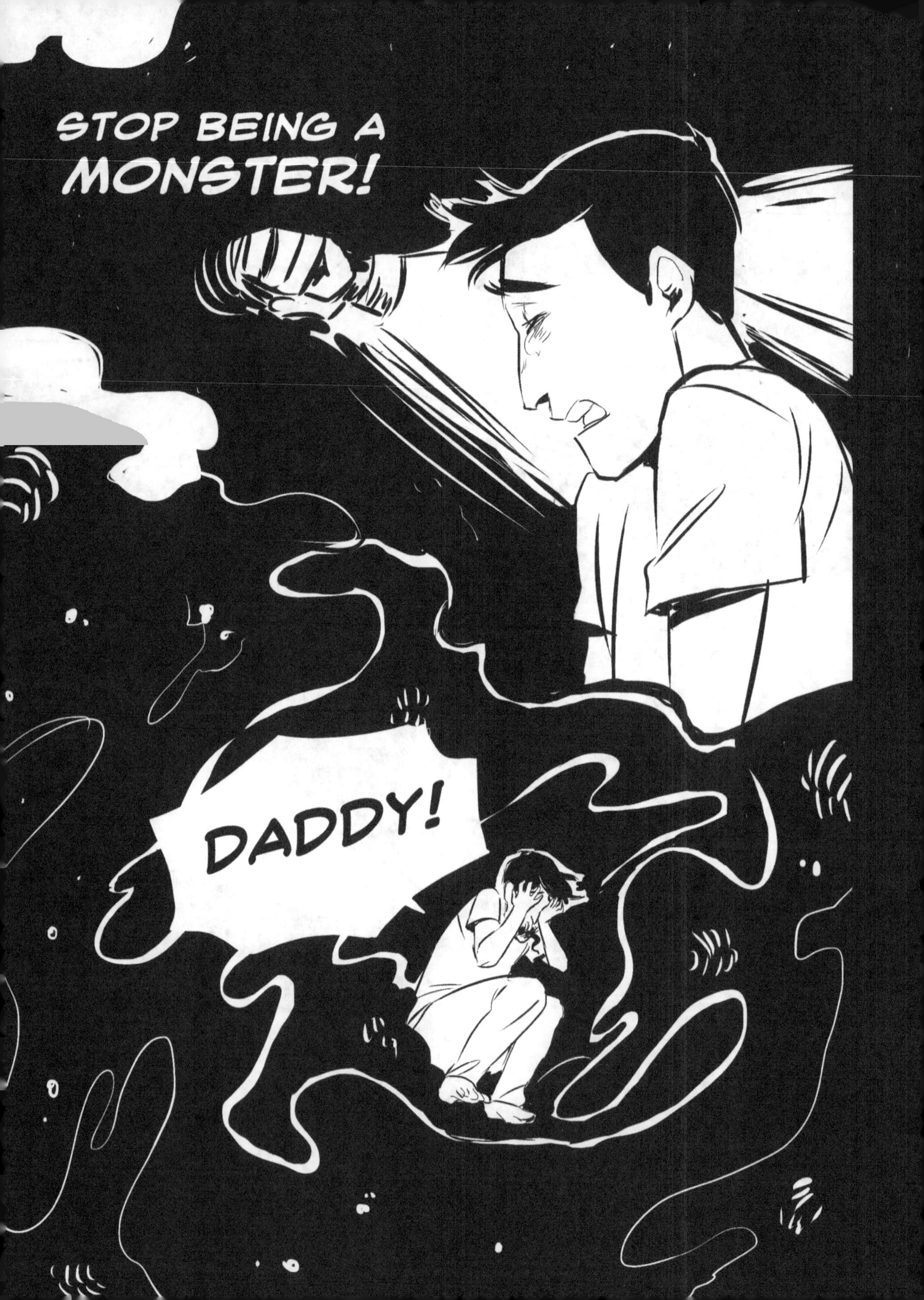
STOP BEING A MONSTER!
DADDY!

HEY...
YOU SLEEPING, BIG GUY?
ATE SOMETHING I WASN'T SUPPOSED TO....
ARE YOU OKAY?

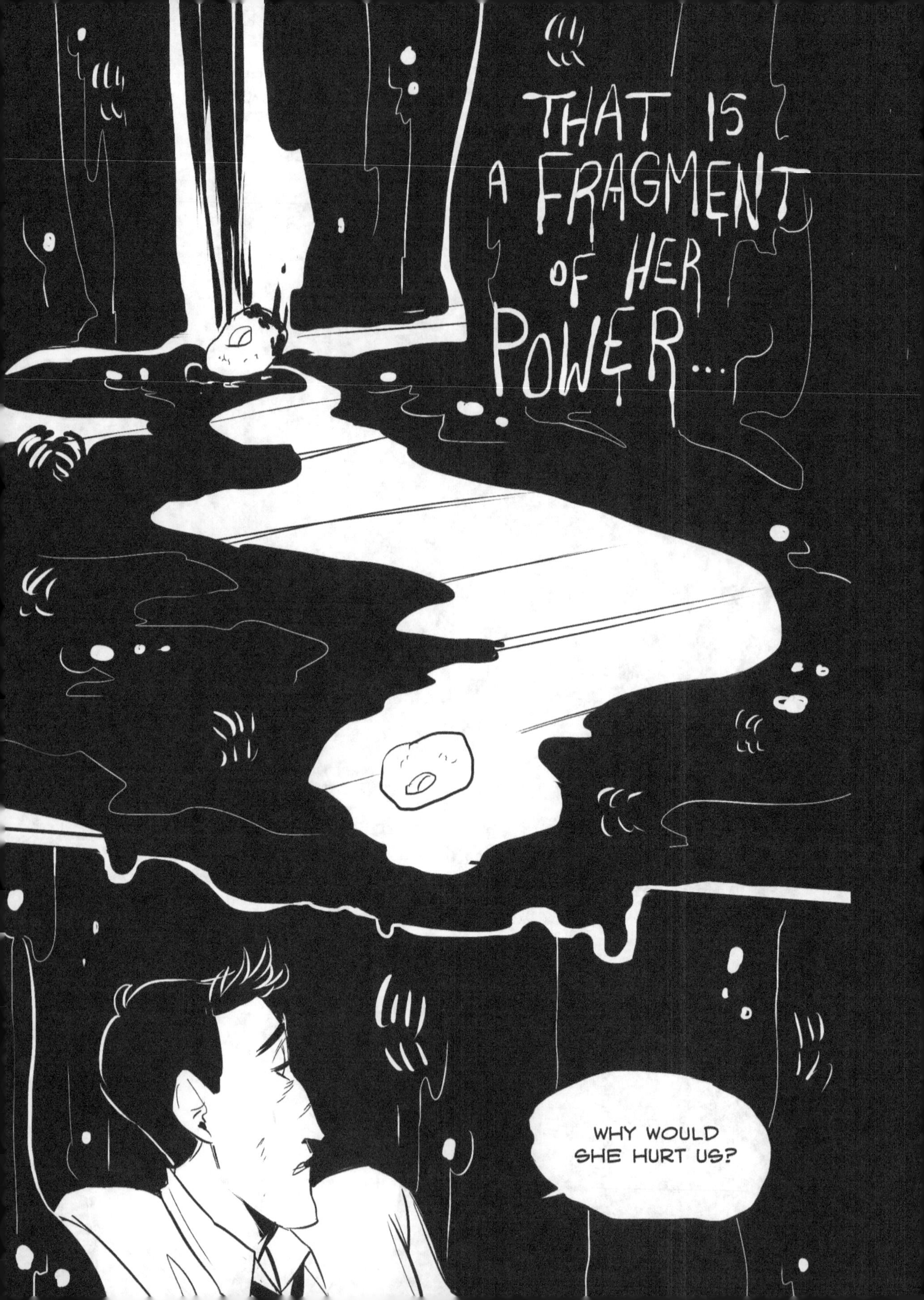
THAT IS A FRAGMENT OF HER POWER...
WHY WOULD SHE HURT US?

BECAUSE I CURSED HER, LONG AGO, WHEN THE CITY WAS YOUNG AND HUMANKIND FEARED WITCHES AND THE MONSTER IN THE WOODS...

I ATE WHAT WANDERED INTO MY MOUTHS AND SHE PREYED...

I CURSED HER, TOOK HER FACE AND LEFT HER A SHADOW ON THE WORLD. NEVER ACKNOWLEDED BY HUMANS, AND NEVER ALLOWED TO TOUCH THEM. UNTIL NOW, SHE WAS NOTHING BUT A GHOST.

I NEED TO STOP CARING.

EVERYONE NEEDS TO.

I'M NOT WORTH IT.

SAY GOOD-BYE, IRA.

YOU CAN BE HUMAN AGAIN.

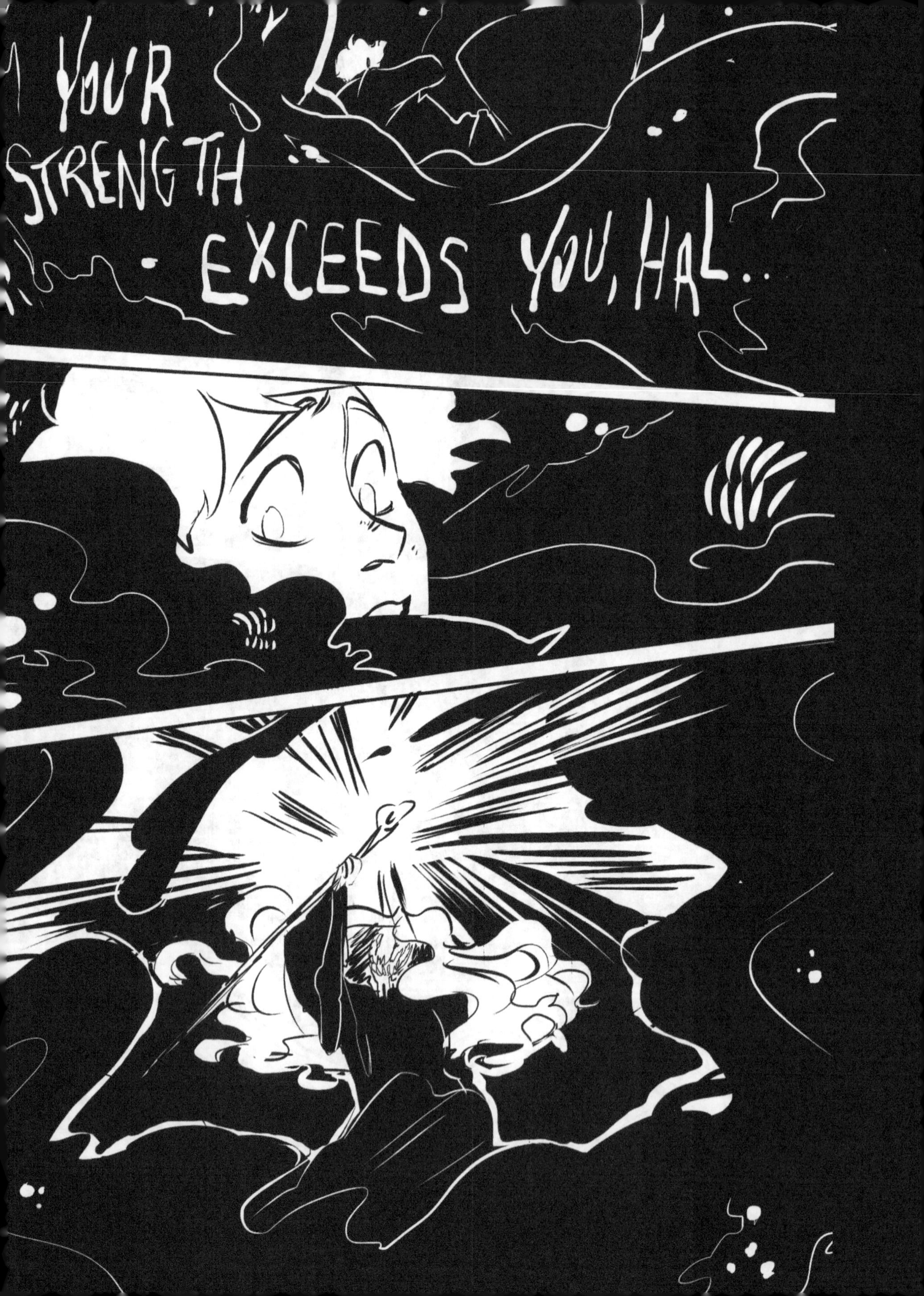
YOUR STRENGTH EXCEEDS YOU, HAL..

....NOTHING IS EVER GOING TO BE OKAY.

FIN.

PRETTY MOUTH
BY
BONES MCKAY
URSULA GRAY

THANK YOU FOR READING!

BONUS CONTENT

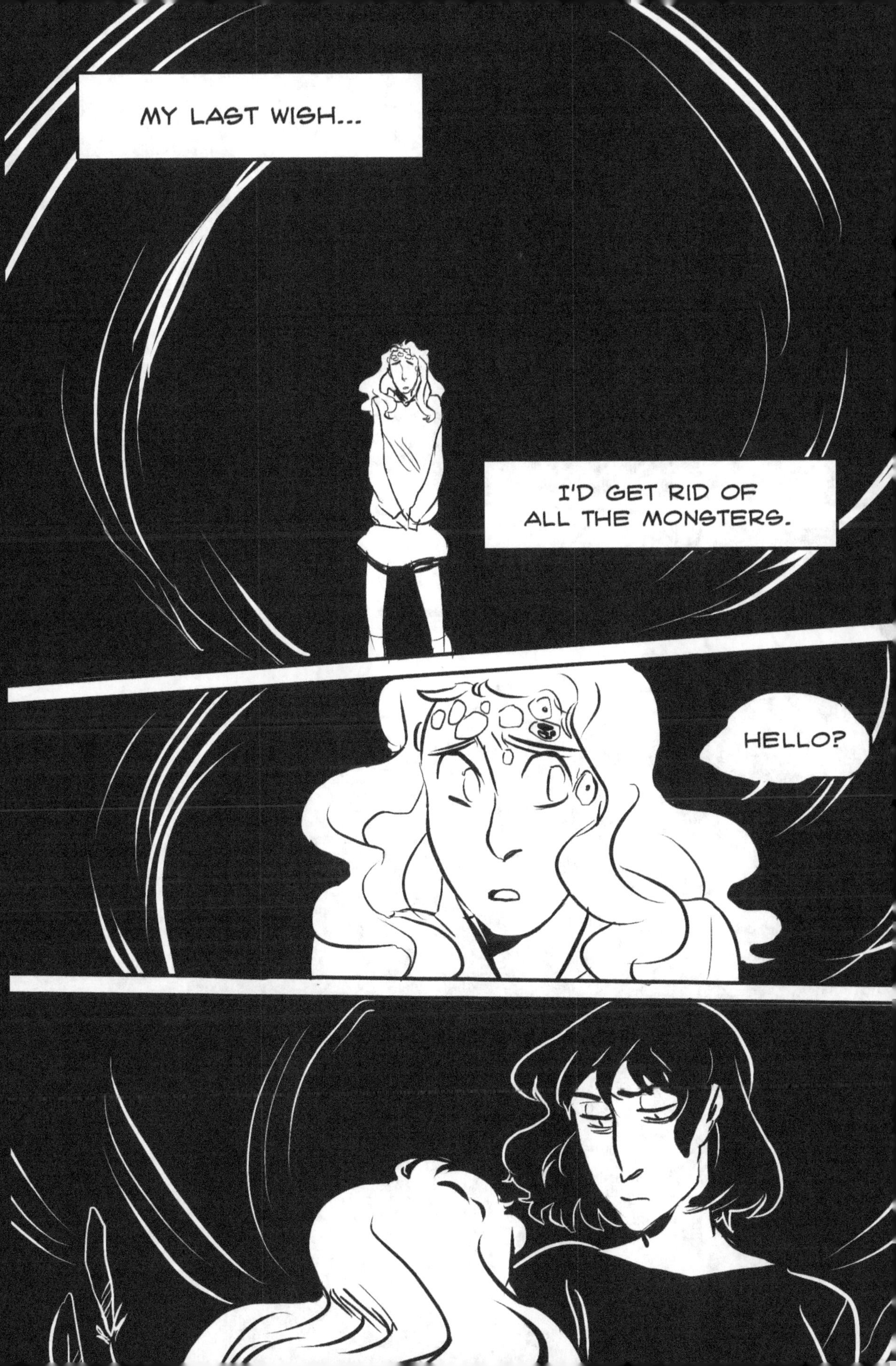
MY LAST WISH...
I'D GET RID OF ALL THE MONSTERS.
HELLO?

MOM TOLD ME,
WE'D LIVE FOREVER.

MY SISTER WAS HUMAN.

I AM NOT HUMAN.

BONUS CONTENT

RIZO AND EVAN, HOW DID YOU TWO MEET?

OH, I WENT TO THE GROCERY STORE AND EVAN WAS THERE. I ASKED HIM IF HE WANTED STEAK.

THEN HE WENT TO MY HOUSE AND THAT'S KIND OF IT.

WHAT HE SAID.

RIZO, COULD YOU TELL US ABOUT YOUR MOM?

MY MOM? UH... I'VE HAD A FEW AND I FEEL REALLY SORRY ABOUT FORGETTING THEM...

I DON'T THINK I WAS LIKED MUCH BY THEM ANYWAYS BECAUSE I SCARED THE OTHER FOSTER CHILDREN.

DO YOU LIKE HUGS?

YES.

HOW OLD ARE YOU TWO?

EVAN HOW DID YOU GET THE MOUTHS?

WHERE IS YOUR TUMMY MOUTH?

RIZO, CAN I PRETTY PLEASE GIVE YOU A HUG?
YOU LOOK LIKE YOU NEED SOME SERIOUS CUDDLES.

URSULA, WHO IS YOUR FAVORITE CHARACTER TO DRAW; IS THERE ANYONE WHO IS EASIER THAN THE OTHERS?

BONES, IN THAT HALLOWEEN STRIP WITH YOUNG RIZO IN THE GHOST COSTUME; WHERE DID HE GET THE OUTFIT?!? DID HIS DAD EAT SOME TRICK-OR-TREATERS OR SOMETHING AND JUST GAVE HIM THE LEFT OVER CLOTHES? (NO MATTER WHAT IT WAS ADORABLE THOUGH).

EVAN, BEFORE THE WHOLE HAVING TO EAT THING WITH RIZO AT HIS PLACE; DID YOU ENJOY THE DATE?

RIZO, HOW COULD YOU POSSIBLY BE THIS GENTLE TOWARD EVAN, AFTER ALL THE PAIN HE MADE YOU FEEL?

RIZO, CAN YOU EAT A PUMPKIN?

DOES EVAN PUT LIPSTICK ON THE PRETTY MOUTH, JUST TO BE NICE?

THIS IS TOO PERSONAL, BUT I WONDER HOW WAS RIZO AND EVAN'S NIGHT TOGETHER? DID THEY DO IT? DID THEY LIKE IT?

DID RIZO HAVE RELATIONS WITH ANY OTHER GUYS BEFORE EVAN?

WHAT KIND OF MUSIC DOES RIZO LIKE?

ARE THEY GONNA KISS?

WHY IS IRA SUCH A JERK?

WHAT DOES SILVER DO FOR FUN?

ARE EVAN AND RIZO GOING TO BE IN A RELATIONSHIP?

TOP LEFT: ORIGINAL DRAWING OF EVAN, RAMONA AND HAL.

LOWER LEFT: ORIGINAL MONSTER DAD DRAWING.

BELOW: RAMONA AND HAL CONCEPTS.

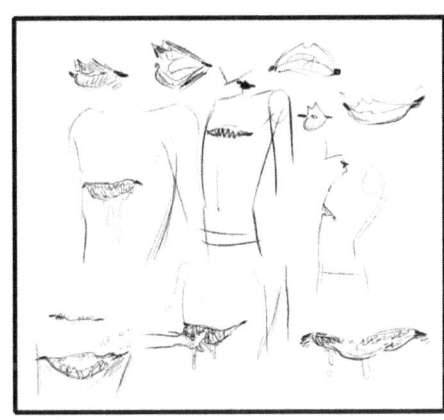

RIGHT: SKETCHES TO DEVELOP RIZO, EVAN, AND SILVER'S DESIGNS.

LEFT: ORIGINAL
RAMONA CONCEPT
SKETCHES.

ABOVE: KRIS, ETHAN,
AND SILVER SKETCH.

BELOW: ORIGINAL IRA
CONCEPT SKETCHES.

ABOVE: HAL'S DESIGN SHEET.

RIGHT: SKETCHES FOR
"THE INFINITE".

BELOW: EVAN, RIZO, SILVER,
AND MONSTER DAD AS CATS,
DRAWN BY BONES.

THE
MAGPIE

TO WHAT I OWE THIS TRIBUTE?
DO
SPEAK WITCH.
WHAT IS IT YOU WANT?
I...UM...

YES. I DO NOT UNDERSTAND.
BUT IF YOU WANT HIM, TAKE HIM. I WILL NEVER FIND WHAT HE SEEKS.
I DO NOT WANT WORTHLESS SACRIFICE ANYMORE.

CONTINUE READING!
PRETTYMOUTHCOMIC.COM

www.ingramcontent.com/pod-product-compliance
Lightning Source LLC
Chambersburg PA
CBHW080953020726
47505CB00009B/2183